MR.
NONSENSE

by Roger Hargreaves

D1454139

Mr Nonsense had no sense at all.

Not a scrap.

I mean, he lived in a tree.

A tree!

Can you imagine?

"Why do you live in a tree?" Mr Happy asked him one day.

"Because," replied Mr Nonsense, "I tried living on the ground, but that was too high up, so I moved to a tree to be nearer the ground."

"What nonsense," snorted Mr Happy.

"Thank you," replied Mr Nonsense.

And, do you know what Mr Nonsense liked to eat?

Porridge!

Nothing wrong with that you might say.

But, porridge on toast!

Really!

"Why do you like porridge on toast?" Mr Nosey asked him one day.

"Because," replied Mr Nonsense, "I tried porridge sandwiches and I didn't like them!"

And, do you know where Mr Nonsense sleeps every night?

In a rowing boat!

In his bedroom.

In his house.

Up a tree.

"Why do you sleep in a rowing boat?" Mr Strong asked him one day.

"Because," replied Mr Nonsense, "I tried sleeping in a motor boat but it was somewhat uncomfortable!"

Mr Nonsense lives, as you might very well expect, in a country called Nonsenseland.

Now, I know somebody else who lives in Nonsenseland.

Do you?

That's right.

Mr Silly!

Mr Silly and Mr Nonsense were close friends and saw a lot of each other.

Mr Nonsense was often round at Mr Silly's house playing jigsaw puzzles.

They used to throw the pieces at each other!

How silly!

And Mr Silly was often round at Mr Nonsense's house playing cards.

They used to tear them up to see who could get the most pieces out of one card!

What nonsense!

However, this story is about the time it snowed in Nonsenseland.

It didn't very often snow, but one winter it did.

Now, tell me, what colour is snow?

No, in Nonsenseland, when it snows, it doesn't snow white snow.

It snows yellow snow!

Don't ask me why.

But it does.

Yellow snow!

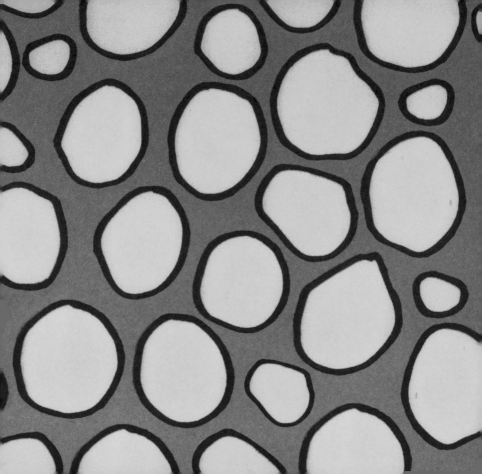

And, when Mr Silly woke up one morning, the whole of Nonsenseland was covered.

"I say," he said when he looked out of his bedroom window. "Snow!"

And he was so excited he rushed round to Mr Nonsense's house.

Mr Nonsense was asleep.

In his boat.

"Wake up!" cried Mr Silly. "Wake up, and come and look out of the window."

"What ever on earth is it?" grumbled Mr Nonsense, rubbing the sleep out of his eyes as he got up and went across to his bedroom window.

"I say," he said, looking out. "Custard!"

"That isn't custard, you silly banana," cried Mr Silly. "That's snow!"

He rushed downstairs.

"Come on," he called.

And that day, Mr Silly and Mr Nonsense had one of the very best days of their lives.

They had a snowball fight.

Mr Silly's snowballs were round.

Mr Nonsense made snowballs that somehow or other came out sort of square!

They built a snowman.

A very silly nonsensical sort of a snowman.

"Come on," said Mr Nonsense that afternoon. "Let's go tobogganing!"

"But we don't have a toboggan," said Mr Silly.

"Oh no, we don't," agreed Mr Nonsense.

Mr Silly thought.

"Oh yes, we do," he cried.

And Mr Silly ran back to Mr Nonsense's house, and came back with his bed.

"Wheeeee!" they shouted together as they slid faster and faster down the hill in their rowing boat toboggan.

It was a wonderful day.

And that evening, after having supper together (porridge pie), Mr Nonsense suggested that they played a game.

"What shall we play?" asked Mr Silly.

"Draughts," suggested Mr Nonsense.

"I've forgotten how to play draughts," said Mr Silly.

"Oh, it's easy," replied Mr Nonsense.

And went round and opened all the doors and windows!

"There we are," he said. "Draughts!"

What nonsense!